Adapted by N. B. Grace
Based on the series created by Dan Povenmire & Jeff "Swampy" Marsh

DISNEY PRESS
New York

Part One

Chapter 1

It was a beautiful summer morning. Phineas Flynn and his stepbrother, Ferb Fletcher, were eating breakfast at their kitchen table. Their friends Django, Buford, and Isabella were there, too. They were all excited because they were headed to the circus in a little while.

Their friend Baljeet burst into the kitchen.

"We're going to the circus! We're going to the circus!" he chanted. He stopped and

smiled at his friends. "I am here and ready to go to the world-famous Cirque du Lune!"

"Have a seat," Phineas said. "We're going in a minute."

"Okay," Baljeet said, trying to contain himself. But he couldn't. Almost immediately, he started chanting again. "We're going to the circus! We're going to the circus!"

Mr. Fletcher walked into the kitchen holding a newspaper. Ferb and his dad were from England. When Mr. Fletcher and Phineas's mom married, Phineas and Ferb had become stepbrothers. But they had never thought of

themselves that way. From the beginning, they had felt as if they were best friends.

"Hold your horses, kids," Mr. Fletcher said, pointing to a newspaper article. "It says here that the lead of Cirque du Lune has a severe allergy. They're canceling today's performance."

"Well, that's a bummer," Isabella said sadly.

Phineas's mom, Mrs. Flynn-Fletcher, walked in carrying a coffee mug. "If it's anything like Candace's parsnip allergy—*whew!*—I  don't blame him for not wanting to appear in public," Mrs. Flynn-Fletcher said.

Candace Flynn was Phineas and Ferb's older sister. She had a very strong reaction to wild parsnips.

"She gets blotchy and red . . . weird-voice thingy," Phineas explained to Isabella. "Not good," he added in a whisper.

Mrs. Flynn-Fletcher turned to her husband. "Well, honey, looks like that frees you up to join me at the mall," she said brightly. "Our trio is recording our first album today: *Live at the Squat 'n' Stitch!*"

Phineas's mom played keyboard in a jazz band with two of her friends. They had been rehearsing for weeks, and they were very excited about their album.

"Mmm-mmm. Should be swinging!" Mr. Fletcher agreed.

Mrs. Flynn-Fletcher hugged Phineas and Ferb. She looked around the table at everyone's sad expressions. "Cheer up, guys," she said. "I'm sure you'll have a fun day anyway." She walked to the door with Mr. Fletcher. "Bye, kids!" she called. "Be good! Have fun!"

Phineas and Ferb's parents left. The five friends looked at each other, a little sad about the change in their plans.

"It must be so cool to be in the circus," Isabella said wistfully.

"Yeah," Phineas agreed. Suddenly he had an idea. "Hey, Ferb, let's put on our own *cirque*!" he cried. He grinned as he realized that, once again, he had come up with a stupendously good plan. "This will be great! Ferb can set up the tent, I'll be the ringmaster—"

"We can sew up some arty costumes!" Isabella suggested.

"For a trick, I can put my leg over my head!" Django offered.

Still sitting down, Django tried to wrap his leg behind his neck. He lost his balance, and he and his chair fell backward onto the floor with a loud *crash*! "*Ow*! I'll work on it."

"Even Perry can have an act. The Amazing Perry!" Phineas shouted, pretending to be a circus ringmaster. Perry was Phineas and Ferb's pet platypus.

Perry looked around, startled. He had been quietly enjoying his own breakfast, which was served in a bowl on the floor. He had not expected to hear himself introduced as if he were a trapeze artist or tightrope walker. At least not this early in the morning.

"Ooh! I have a mystical, magical act I would like to perform," Baljeet said. He

clasped his hands together, then moved them apart. He kept one thumb tucked behind his palm, making it look as if it had disappeared. "It's stupefying!" he shouted.

Buford watched Baljeet's trick. Buford usually acted tough, but even he was caught up in the excitement.

"I have an act that'll bring the house down," Buford said proudly.

Phineas could not wait to put their plan into action. "Ferb, get the tools!" he shouted.

"Let's do this!" Isabella cried.

"Great!" Django agreed.

"*Woo-hoo!*" Baljeet called.

The group rushed out the kitchen door and into the backyard. They had a lot to do if they were going to put on their very own circus.

Upstairs in her bed, Phineas and Ferb's older sister, Candace, had just woken up. She stretched and yawned. She smiled at a framed photo on the pillow next to hers. It was of Jeremy Johnson, the boy she liked.

"Good morning, Jeremy!" Candace said to the photograph. She pretended to be Jeremy and answered in a deep voice. "Good morning, gorgeous." She giggled. "Oh, Jer!"

She picked up a framed photo of herself. Then she held the two pictures together and made kissing noises.

Suddenly, there was a loud buzzing sound outside.

"I'll be right back, Jeremy," Candace said, frowning. She jumped out of bed and went to her bedroom window. "What's going on?" she said.

Just then, a huge pink-and-purple circus tent rose in the backyard.

"A circus?!" Candace cried. "Why can't they give me a break for one day?"

This was just like Phineas and Ferb, Candace thought. They were always trying out crazy schemes, from entering a car race to building a roller coaster in the backyard. The

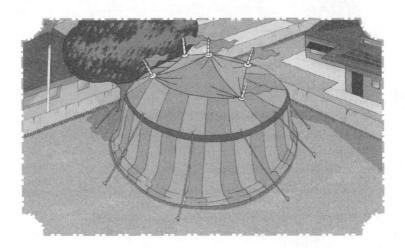

most irritating part to Candace was that her brothers always got away with them. Their parents never suspected a thing! It looked as if today would be no different.

Chapter 2

Inside the big-top tent, Phineas and Ferb's friends were trying out their acts and setting up bleachers. Phineas was dressed as a ringmaster. He wore a top hat, orange pants, and a bright blue jacket with gold trim. Ferb had on a green hat with bells, a green-and-purple outfit, and clown makeup. He was dressed as a jester.

Phineas looked around. "This looks great,

Ferb!" he said. "Hey, have you seen Perry? I put on his costume."

Perry the Platypus may have been wearing a costume, but he was not happy about it. He had on a top made of two coconut halves, a ruffled skirt, and a black mask. Four green feathers were attached to his head.

Although Perry was dressed for a circus, he was not going to wait around to take part in it. That's because he was more than just a platypus. He was also a secret agent who

worked for a secret organization to fight a secret enemy. It was all so secret that even Phineas and Ferb didn't know Perry's true identity. They thought Perry was just a pet.

Outside the tent, Perry trotted across the backyard toward a secret transportation device. He stopped, and a glass elevator rose out of a section of the lawn. Perry stepped inside and pushed a button. The elevator quickly sank into a tunnel that led to Perry's secret-agent hideout.

A short while later, Perry sat in a chair in front of a large monitor. His boss, Major Monogram, appeared on-screen.

Major Monogram had a mustache and wore a military uniform. He usually looked very

serious. When he looked up from his report and saw Perry wearing his ridiculous circus costume, he started to laugh. He managed to control his laughter long enough to speak.

"Okay, Agent P," Major Monogram said, "Dr. Doofenshmirtz is buying biomechanical equipment and elocution tapes."

Then he started laughing even harder. "We—we don't know why."

Annoyed, Perry stood up and headed for the door.

"W—where are you going, Agent P?" Major

Monogram asked. "Wait, wait, wait, wait. Don't go. I'm not laughing at you. I—I just heard a funny joke earlier this morning and . . ."

Perry stopped walking, but he didn't look back at the monitor. Major Monogram was going to have to do better than that if he wanted Perry to stay.

"Please. Please, Agent P, turn around so we can conclude our meeting," the major said.

Perry hesitated. His feelings were hurt, but his old foe, Dr. Doofenshmirtz, was up to no good! The fate of the world was more important than his feelings, Perry decided.

He faced the monitor again. Just then, Major Monogram held up his cell phone and took a picture of Perry. He started laughing again.

"Karl, what's your e-mail?" he called off-screen. "I'm going to send this to you."

Disgusted, Perry walked out. Major Monogram was still chuckling.

At the big-top tent, Buford was preparing for his own mission—his circus act. He pushed a cart full of equipment toward the tent entrance, where Phineas was standing.

"Hey, twerp, I brought the props for my act," Buford said.

Phineas looked at the cart, which was filled

with wooden boards and a large metal spring.

"Buford, what exactly is your act?" Phineas asked.

"I fly into mud with a paper bag on my head," Buford said proudly. He held up a hand-drawn diagram that showed a catapult made of the boards and spring. The diagram also showed a huge tub of mud.

Phineas blinked. Being thrown into a vat of mud did not sound like his idea of a good time. Of course, he wasn't Buford. He wasn't interested in arguing, either.

"Okay, then," Phineas said with a nod.

"The peeps are going to *lo-ove* this," Buford said as he pushed his cart into the tent.

Meanwhile, Candace had gotten dressed. She walked outside and stared at the tent, which looked even bigger up close. "I'm not even going to call Mom," she murmured. "No, not going to call."

Then she heard what sounded like an elephant inside the tent. An elephant?! Candace thought. What if it got loose and went on a rampage? What if it trampled flowerbeds and little kids' tricycles? This time Phineas and Ferb had gone too far.

Candace whipped out her cell phone and dialed her mother.

"Candace, honey, listen, I can't talk," Mrs. Flynn-Fletcher said over the phone. "We're recording. Is it life or death?"

Candace looked at the circus tent. If there was an elephant, it hadn't gone on a rampage—yet.

"Well, no," she said. "But—"

"Then I've got to go!" her mother interrupted. "Bye!"

Candace groaned in frustration. Just then, Jeremy walked up holding a basket of vegetables.

"Hey, Candace," he said.

"Oh! Hi, Jeremy!" Candace said happily.

"My mom told me to bring over these home-grown veggies for your family," Jeremy said. "You know, she and your mom are doing that jazz thing today."

Candace tried to think of something witty to say. She wanted to impress Jeremy, but her mind was blank. So she just smiled. "Thanks."

Jeremy looked at the tent. "So, a circus? Cool." He paused. "I guess it's more of a *cirque* than a circus." He chuckled.

Candace rubbed her nose, which was starting to itch. It didn't bother her because Jeremy was standing next to her. And talking to her! And breathing the same air as her!

She sighed dreamily as she looked at Jeremy's blond hair and blue eyes. His face was framed by a beautiful summer sky. Candace imagined she could hear voices singing in the background. Jeremy turned to her and spoke. Candace thought she heard, "Good morning, gorgeous."

"Oh!" she said, giggling.

"Don't you think?" Jeremy asked.

Candace snapped back to reality. "What?" she asked.

"Don't you think we should sit together?" Jeremy repeated. "To watch the show? If—if you want to . . ."

Candace couldn't believe it. Jeremy was asking to sit next to *her* at the circus. It was almost as if he were asking her on a date!

"Yeah! Yeah!" Candace said. But, suddenly, she started to cough.

"Uh, Candace, are you okay?" Jeremy asked, looking worried.

Candace abruptly fell to the ground. Her face was covered with red splotches.

She looked at the basket of vegetables she was holding. An awful thought occurred to her. "Say, are there any wild parsnips in here?"

"Uh, I think that's all that's in there," Jeremy said, confused.

Of course, Candace thought. Wild parsnips, which I'm completely allergic to. She stood up, leaving the basket on the ground.

"Later!" Candace said. Still coughing, she quickly staggered away.

She had to get rid of this allergy—fast—if she wanted to sit next to Jeremy at the circus.

Chapter 3

Agent P was on his way to his enemy's secret hideout. He was determined to uncover Dr. Doofenshmirtz's latest evil plan.

Meanwhile, inside Dr. Doofenshmirtz's headquarters, the scientist was listening to a tape called *Tuff Talk*. The recorded male voice sounded as if he wanted to get into a fight.

"I'm dancing with your wife, pal!" the voice said angrily. "You got a problem with that?"

Dr. Doofenshmirtz listened carefully. Then he tried to repeat the sentence in a tough-sounding voice.

"'I'm dan—'" Dr. Doofenshmirtz began, but his voice came out high and squeaky. He cleared his throat and tried again. "'I'm dancing with your wife, pal! You got a problem with that?'" This time he sounded angry.

He gasped with delight. "Oh, yes, that does sound tough!"

The voice on the tape went on. "Yeah, I ate your last nectarine. You got a problem with that?"

Eagerly, Dr. Doofenshmirtz started to repeat the line. "'Yes, I ate—'"

At that moment, Perry crashed through the ceiling! He was flying with a portable propeller. He had changed out of his circus costume and was now wearing his secret-agent hat, a brown fedora.

"Perry the Platypus!" Dr. Doofenshmirtz said.

26

"Look, could—" Dust from the smashed-in ceiling surrounded the scientist. *Cough! Cough!* "Could you just use the front door from now on? Could you just do that for me?"

Perry glanced at the front door. Right in front of it was a large steel trap. As if the famous Agent P would fall for a trick like that! Perry thought.

Dr. Doofenshmirtz realized he hadn't sounded tough at all. In fact, he had sounded a little whiny.

He cleared his throat. "Yes, I ate your last nectarine," he said to Perry in a threatening tone. "You got a problem with that?"

Confused, Perry stared at his enemy.

"Sounds tough, huh?" Dr. Doofenshmirtz said, nodding. "But not tough enough."

He held up a remote control and pushed a large red button. A net fell from the ceiling and landed on Perry! Trapped inside, the platypus was yanked into the air.

"You see, ever since I was a child, I have had a high, squeaky voice," said Dr. Doofenshmirtz. "But not anymore. Behold, the Voice-inator!" He pointed to a huge machine. "It biomechanically transforms normal air into *Doofelium*, which will make everyone else's voice higher, making my voice deeper by comparison," he explained. "I was going to lower my own voice, but, you know, it seemed like too much trouble."

The scientist climbed onto the Voice-inator and started the engine. The machine blasted

off the ground toward the hole in the ceiling.

As he steered the machine through the roof, even more rubble and dust fell into Dr. Doofenshmirtz's headquarters. "Oh, come on!" he cried in disgust.

Still trapped inside the net, Perry watched the evil scientist fly away on his invention. Perry's mission was now clear: to stop Dr. Doofenshmirtz from using the Voice-inator on the world!

In her bedroom, Candace was trying to stop a disaster of her own. She sat down at her dressing table and stared into the mirror. Her face was red, swollen, and covered in splotches.

"Of course, it had to be wild parsnips!" Candace said with a groan.

She opened a drawer and frantically searched. "Allergy pills, allergy pills . . ." she muttered. Finally, she spotted a medicine bottle. "*Ah-ha!* Quick, before my voice goes through the reaction!"

Candace opened the bottle and shook it—but it was empty!

"*No!*" she cried. When she heard her unnaturally deep voice, she realized it was already too late.

Then she heard a girl's voice outside her window.

"Hey, Jeremy! Want to sit together at the show?"

Candace ran to her window and looked out. A girl from school named Mindy stood on the sidewalk, talking to Jeremy.

"No! No! Mindy can't sit with Jeremy!" Candace growled in her new, deep voice. "Got to stop this! Got to tell Mom!"

Candace suddenly saw her reflection in the window. She put her hands to her face, which was covered with splotches. "Can't go out looking like this!"

As Candace looked around her room, she saw a paper bag on the floor. She had an idea. . . .

A few moments later, Candace snuck out of her house. She had put the paper bag over her head to disguise herself. She spotted Mindy and Jeremy and tried to edge past them without being seen.

"So how about us sitting together?" Mindy said to Jeremy.

Candace forgot about sneaking past. Instead, she ran toward Mindy and shoved her aside.

" 'Scuse me," she said with a growl.

"Oh, it's good, bro," Jeremy said.

Candice was stunned. Jeremy thought she was just some strange guy wearing a paper bag! Upset, Candace hurried away.

After she had run off, Jeremy turned back to Mindy.

"Thanks," he said politely, "but I promised Candace."

Meanwhile, Perry was still trapped in Dr. Doofenshmirtz's lab. Inside the net, Perry took off his fedora. He pulled a cord that started up a saw hidden inside. He used the

saw to cut the net, then jumped to the ground.

Moments later, he was flying his portable propeller toward home.

When Perry flew over the Flynn-Fletchers' backyard, he heard Phineas's voice boom out over a loudspeaker. "We're moments away from Ferb and the Amazing Perry!"

Perry sighed. Dr. Doofenshmirtz planned to change the voice of every person in the world. If he wasn't stopped, everyone would sound as squeaky as the evil doctor. Perry had a duty

33

to stop him. But he also had a duty to his owners, Phineas and Ferb.

Perry pulled out his coconut-shell top and steered toward the backyard.

Inside the big top, the bleachers were filled. Three circus rings had been set up. In the center ring, Baljeet was peforming his thumb trick. Phineas and Ferb watched from the sidelines.

Phineas turned to his stepbrother. "Hey, Ferb, you guys are up next. Where's Perry?" Then he spotted the platypus. "Oh, there you are!"

Baljeet continued his act. "And now, for my final trick," he said to the audience. "I will reattach my thumb. Feel the rhythm! Feel the rhyme! Come on, thumb, it's healing time!"

With a quick movement, Baljeet made it look as if his thumb was now reattached. He held up his hands in triumph. Ferb hit a beat on his drum kit. The audience cheered.

"Let's hear it for Baljeet the Stupefying!" Phineas said into his microphone. "But now, prepare to be astounded when the Amazing Semiaquatic Perry, aided by Ferb, attempts to jump through that hoop into the shallow pond!" Phineas pointed toward the center ring.

"Ooh! Aah!" called the audience.

A spotlight lit up a platform where Ferb stood holding Perry. A trampoline, a large hoop, and a small swimming pool were lined up in front of the platform. Ferb didn't hesitate. He knew Perry could do this stunt, even without a rehearsal.

35

On the platform, Ferb held out his arms and dropped Perry. The platypus bounced on the trampoline, jumped through the hoop, and landed in the pool of water with barely a splash. The stunt had gone off perfectly.

"Yeah! Let's hear it for the Amazing Semiaquatic Perry!" Phineas yelled into his microphone. Cheers filled the circus tent.

His performance finished, Perry was free to go back to his real work—fighting crime. He ducked out of the circus tent. His portable propeller was still hovering in the air. He grabbed the handles and flew off. It was time to stop Dr. Doofenshmirtz!

Chapter 4

After running away from Jeremy and Mindy, Candace had decided to go tell her mother about Phineas and Ferb's circus. Still wearing the paper bag, Candace hopped a bus to the mall in order to track down her mother.

Mrs. Flynn-Fletcher and her jazz group were in the Squat 'n' Stitch when Candace found them.

"*Psst!* Mom!" Candace whispered huskily.

Mrs. Flynn-Fletcher recognized her daughter's voice without even turning around. "Candace, have you been near the wild parsnips again?"

Candace rolled her eyes. She had almost forgotten about her allergy after seeing what her little brothers were up to in the backyard. "Yes, but you've got to see what Phineas and Ferb are doing!"

"What is it now?" her mother said with a sigh. She fiddled with the settings on her electronic keyboard.

Candace realized that her mother was much more interested in music than in Phineas and Ferb's latest scheme. So Candace began to sing. Because of her allergy, her voice sounded more like a growl.

Candace sang about her brothers' past schemes, including when they built a roller coaster and a beach in the backyard. She sang about the time they built a fifty-foot tree-house robot but didn't get in trouble because their parents never saw it.

One of Mrs. Flynn-Fletcher's friends, Mrs. Garcia-Shapiro, was strumming on her bass guitar. "Testify, Candace!" she yelled, impressed by her passionate performance. "Testify!"

Encouraged, Candace grabbed a microphone. Then she wiped off a dry-erase board on the wall. As she sang, she wrote the words EVIL BOYS on the board.

Mrs. Flynn-Fletcher thought her daughter was giving a great performance. She picked up her guitar and plugged it in. She began playing

some blues riffs to back up Candace, who continued to sing.

In the audience, Mr. Fletcher adjusted the sound levels on his recording equipment. The women in the knitting class bobbed their heads to the music without missing a stitch.

Candace sang another verse about her brothers. The women in the knitting class sang

along with the chorus. The second time they sang, the women held up their knitting. They had knitted the letters EVIL BOYS, to go along with Candace's song.

Candace dropped to her knees for a

big finish and belted out the last line.

At the end of the song, the women in the knitting class cheered and threw balls of red yarn into the air.

A little breathless, Candace turned to her mother. "So are you going to come home with me?"

Mrs. Flynn-Fletcher smiled at her. "Are you kidding, hon?" she cried. "Let's do another!"

Candace groaned.

Using his portable propeller, Perry flew to where the Voice-inator was sailing through the sky. He landed on the deck in front of Dr. Doofenshmirtz.

"Perry the Platypus," Dr. Doofenshmirtz cried. "You are too late!"

Perry saw a large switch that was labeled ON/OFF. He reached for it.

"Wait!" Dr. Doofenshmirtz slapped Perry's paw away.

It would take more than that to stop Agent P! Perry reached toward the switch again.

"Wait, don't touch that!" Dr. Doofenshmirtz yelled, knocking Perry's paw away once more.

Perry tried again. For the next few minutes, he tried to turn off the switch, and Dr. Doofenshmirtz slapped at his paw.

"Stop it, stop it! Stop it, I told you!" Dr. Doofenshmirtz shouted over and over.

Finally, the scientist tried to just cover the switch with his hands.

Perry was ready. He started to tickle Dr. Doofenshmirtz.

Dr. Doofenshmirtz giggled helplessly. "Stop—stop it!" he cried. "Stop it!"

Perry tickled him even more. The scientist laughed so hard that he lost his grip. Perry saw his chance and reached for the switch.

"I said keep your hands off that!" Dr. Doofenshmirtz yelled.

Perry lunged for the switch. It was his only chance.

Back at their circus, Phineas and Ferb watched the latest act. A half-dozen girls stood in a pyramid on each other's shoulders twirling rings on their arms. As they finished, Phineas smiled. All of the acts so far had been terrific!

Buford strolled up, ready to take his place in the spotlight.

"Hey, I've got my costume all set," he said.

"Be sure to introduce me as the 'Amazing Baggo.'"

"You know, we've been thinking about your act and have some suggestions," Phineas said.

Ferb held up a diagram. It was similar to the one that Buford had drawn, except it was much more complicated.

Phineas saw the confused look on Buford's face. "Modify your torque and reverse the angle of trajectory," Phineas explained as he pointed to the diagram.

Buford frowned. "I still get to land in the mud, right?"

"Oh, yeah, yeah!" Phineas said.

"I want the mud," Buford said, in case that point wasn't totally clear.

Phineas and Ferb nodded. They had guessed as much.

A few moments later, Django finished his circus act. He had tried very hard to place his legs behind his head, and now he was all tangled up.

Phineas ran back into the center ring. "Thank you, Django, the human pretzel!"

he cried as Django was loaded into a cart and pushed out of the ring.

"That's got to hurt," Phineas said. "And now, our next act will catapult through the heavens and land in a pit filled

with the mysterious Aztec Mud of Doom!"

The members of the audience sat up a little straighter. This sounded good.

Just then, Candace dashed into the tent. She glanced around at the crowd. When she saw Jeremy sitting next to an empty seat, she almost fainted.

"Jeremy! Jeremy! Jeremy!" she said happily. "He saved a seat for me!"

Phineas looked around the tent for Buford. It was time for his act. Phineas saw Candace wearing a paper bag over her head and thought that she was Buford.

"I give you, the Amazing Baggo!" Phineas yelled. He pushed Candace toward the catapult. She was so surprised that she was unable to talk.

Buford ran toward the ring. "Ta-da!" he cried. He couldn't wait to land in the huge tub of mud. Then he saw that someone else was strapped to the catapult.

"Hey!" Buford yelled.

Candace had been trying to convince her brothers that she wasn't Buford. But her voice was now so deep that they didn't believe her. She struggled to escape from the catapult. Candace wasn't sure what the machine did, but knowing her brothers, it couldn't be good.

"Guys, cut it out!" she yelled. "Let go!"

"That dude's stealing my act!" Buford yelled. The catapult and the mud were *his* ideas! Buford started toward the center ring.

It was too late. Phineas and Ferb pulled the lever. The catapult arm whipped forward.

Candace flew through the air—and out the top of the circus tent!

The crowd stared at the hole in the big top, confused. Ferb whistled in astonishment.

"*Hmmm. . . .* He must have been lighter than we calculated," Phineas said.

"No, no! This is Buford's moment to shine," Buford yelled.

Determined to finish his act, Buford decided to skip the part where he flew through the air. He ran over to the mud pit and jumped in.

"Hey, everybody!" he shouted, waving to the audience. "Over here!"

The audience cheered loudly.

Phineas did a double take. "Wait. How did he get down there?"

"Um, perhaps Buford truly is amazing?" Ferb suggested.

The two brothers considered this, then went to pull Buford out of the mud.

49

Meanwhile, back on the flying Voice-inator, Perry was still fighting Dr. Doofenshmirtz. They struggled back and forth, each trying to gain control of the switch. Then the scientist crashed into it.

CRACK! The switch broke.

"Whoa! Ooh!" Dr. Doofenshmirtz said. He stared at the lever in disgust. "Oh, great. Now this thing is broken!"

Neither Perry nor Dr. Doofenshmirtz realized that when the switch had been hit, a hose detached from the Voice-inator. The hose swung through the air. Then it dropped through the hole in the top of Phineas and Ferb's circus tent. Within moments, Dr. Doofenshmirtz's invention had

transformed the air inside the tent into *Doofelium*.

Inside the big top, no one realized that they were breathing *Doofelium* instead of air. At least, until they starting speaking.

"And now, ladies and gentlemen," Phineas announced in a high-pitched voice, "I give you our entire cast in our grand finale! Featuring the amazing Perry!"

In the sky, Perry heard his cue over the loudspeaker. He grabbed hold of his propeller and flew down into the tent. There, he joined Phineas and Ferb for the finale.

51

Everyone who had performed in the circus formed a human ladder. Since he was larger than the others, Buford was on the bottom. Phineas and Ferb were on his shoulders, and the ring-twirling girls stood on the brothers' shoulders. The tower of kids reached all the way to the top of the tent.

Phineas and Ferb climbed to the very top of the human ladder, where they sat on a trapeze next to Perry.

It was an amazing finale to the circus. Except it was about to get even better. The tent continued to fill up with *Doofelium* gas until it looked as if it were a balloon about to explode. The sides of the tent tugged against the stakes that were holding it to the ground.

Then the stakes pulled free! The tent lifted off the ground, leaving the circus ring, the audience, and all the performers behind.

The tent flew into the sky, where it smashed

into the Voice-inator with a loud *crash*!

Still inside the circus ring with Phineas and Ferb, Perry watched the Voice-inator fall from the sky to the ground. The audience whistled and cheered.

Dr. Doofenshmirtz's voice could be heard in the distance. "Curse you, Perry the Platypus!" he yelled, his voice sounding even squeakier than usual.

Perry shrugged. He hadn't meant for the big top to crash into the Voice-inator, but he was glad that the machine had been destroyed. Now the world was safe again—at least until Dr. Doofenshmirtz's next evil plan!

Chapter 5

As the crowd filed out of the Flynn-Fletchers' backyard, they talked about how great the show was, especially the amazing finale.

"Whoa!" said one boy. "Thanks, Phineas!"

"I thought your *cirque* rocked," added another boy.

"That was awesome!"

"You're the coolest!"

"That was the best circus I've ever been to!"

Isabella smiled in agreement. "Well, Phineas, awesome as usual!"

After the audience left, Phineas and Ferb took apart the circus ring. Then Ferb pulled a lever to lower the circus seats into the ground.

At that moment, Phineas and Ferb's parents returned home. They saw a backyard that looked . . . totally normal.

"Hi, guys!" said Mrs. Flynn-Fletcher.

Phineas waved cheerfully. "Mom, Dad, you missed our *cirque!*"

"Well, it sure looks like you had fun," his mom said as she looked at Perry, who was dressed once again in his circus costume.

Perry grunted, looking unhappy.

Mrs. Flynn-Fletcher held a disc in the air. "Who wants to hear my CD?" she asked.

"*Ooh,* I do!" Phineas said eagerly.

"All right," Mr. Fletcher said. "Come on!"
"Cool!" Ferb exclaimed.

Later that day, the backyard was empty when Candace finally arrived home. After being thrown from the catapult, she had landed a long way from her house. By the time she made it back, she had scratches all over her body and her clothes were torn. Luckily, her face wasn't blotchy and her voice was no longer a deep growl. Her allergic reaction had finally gone away.

"Oh, well, at least I'm back to normal," she said with a sigh.

A shadow fell over her. She looked up to see Jeremy standing beside her, holding a CD.

"Hey, Candace!" he said. "My mom played me some of their CD. Your singing is awesome! How'd you get your voice to sound like that?"

Candace smiled and shrugged. "Oh, same as all the great blues singers—wild parsnips."

Jeremy looked confused, but Candace didn't have the energy to explain. She smiled at Jeremy and headed inside. It could wait for another day—one that hadn't involved a circus in the backyard or a sky-high catapult.

Part Two

Chapter 1

The sun had barely risen, but at exactly 6:59 a.m. Phineas and Ferb sat bolt upright in bed. After all, it was summer. They couldn't waste time by sleeping in.

The clock's display changed to 7:00 a.m. The alarm buzzed loudly. Phineas reached over and turned it off with a look of triumph.

"Beat you to it again, slowpoke!" he said, laughing. "Hey, Ferb, ready to build the

fastest, safest, most on-time backyard railroad ever?"

Ferb clapped a railroad engineer's hat on his head in response. Then he threw off his covers to show that he was already wearing an engineer's uniform.

"All right!" Phineas cried.

The two boys jumped out of bed. They slid down the staircase banister, one after the other.

"You man the boiler. I'll handle the brakes," Phineas said.

The boys ran outside. Ferb saw their pet platypus, Perry, and put his engineer cap on Perry's head.

"Perry can be the station mascot," Phineas said.

Perry made a chattering noise. He would be their mascot—as long as he didn't have more important things to do, of course.

Usually, a beautiful summer day filled Phineas with energy. As soon as he woke up, he would get tons of ideas for projects. But today seemed different somehow.

"Wow, it's really nice out today," Phineas

63

said. "It's almost like everything in nature is simultaneously saying . . ."

He paused to listen and watch. He saw a squirrel sigh and lazily drape itself over a tree branch.

In the yard, a bird was relaxing on a branch. A worm lay on the bird's stomach. Both bird and worm seemed to have forgotten that a worm was usually a bird's lunch.

A spider in its web looked peaceful and

calm. The flies that had been caught in the spiderweb seemed relaxed. Bugs crawling through the grass seemed to sigh happily, too.

Phineas realized that the whole world seemed to be taking the day off! Maybe the world was sending them a message, he thought.

"You know, Ferb," Phineas said, "every day we do something really big, but you know the one thing we haven't done?"

Ferb shook his head.

"Relax," Phineas said. "I say we take advantage of this perfect day and have the best do-nothing day ever!"

Upstairs in her bedroom, Phineas and Ferb's sister, Candace, was planning her day, too. She was talking on her cell phone to her best friend, Stacy.

"Hey, Stacy," Candace said. "Yes! Yes, I'm

ready for Jeremy's band's outdoor concert at the summer festival!"

Candace looked at a copy of the concert program. It read "Jeremy and the Incidentals." The lead singer of the band, Jeremy, happened to be a boy that Candace liked—a lot.

"Today is going to be amazing!" she said.

Candace hung up her phone and looked at her clock. She realized it was nine in the morning—and everything was quiet. Candace sniffed the air suspiciously. Then she licked

her index finger and held it up to check the wind's direction.

"All right, what gives?" she said. "It's already nine o'clock and there's no construction noise, no delivery trucks, no . . ."

She looked out the window. Phineas and Ferb were standing in the backyard, looking innocent.

"They're just standing there," Candace said, puzzled. "Like statues. Like . . ."

That was the answer, Candace thought. They looked like statues! She imagined what must have happened.

"Good thinking, Ferb," Phineas probably said. "We'll put these decoys up so Candace thinks we're doing nothing."

She thought of Phineas and Ferb setting up statues that looked exactly like them, then sneaking off.

"And then while Candace isn't looking, we'll do something!" Phineas probably said.

Then, Candace thought, he would have laughed evilly.

With a gasp, Candace snapped out of her daydream and came back to reality. She knew from experience that nothing was beyond Phineas and Ferb. She was convinced they were planning yet another outrageous scheme.

"Not today, they won't," Candace vowed. She was determined to finally catch her brothers in the act.

In the backyard, Mrs. Flynn-Fletcher walked up to Phineas and Ferb. "Hi, boys,"

she said brightly. "What are you doing?"

"We're doing nothing today," Phineas explained.

"Well, I'm off to the festival to set up my tea-cozy stand," she said, nodding. "Bye!"

"Bye, Mom," Phineas said. He looked around. "Hey, where's Perry?"

Perry had left the backyard. He knew he couldn't afford to do nothing all day. After all, he wasn't just a pet platypus. He was also Agent P, a secret agent of great cunning and skill.

Perry walked over to a garbage can, which was actually the entrance to a hidden passage. He glanced around, then put on his secret-agent hat, a brown fedora. He opened a door in

the side of the garbage can and stepped through it.

Perry slid down a chute to his secret-agent headquarters. He landed in a chair in front of a large TV screen. Usually, Perry would find his boss, Major Monogram, on-screen, ready to tell him about his latest assignment.

Today, the screen showed Major Monogram dancing with a crowd of people under a sparkling disco ball. He was wearing a Hawaiian shirt and looked as if he were having a great time.

Major Monogram caught sight of Perry, who was staring at the screen with surprise.

"Hey, Agent P," said Major Monogram, a little embarrassed. "Karl, give me a close-up."

Suddenly, Major Monogram's face filled the screen. The dance music stopped.

"So, uh, anyway . . . stop Doofenshmirtz," he said with a serious expression. Then he added happily, "Hit it, Karl!"

The music started playing. Major Monogram went back to dancing.

Perry knew that, once again, he had to stop Dr. Doofenshmirtz's latest evil plot. The major hadn't given him much to go on, but Perry knew one thing for sure: if Doofenshmirtz was involved, the world was in grave danger!

Chapter 2

Candace walked into the backyard and looked around. She saw Phineas and Ferb standing under a tree.

"Hi, Candace," Phineas said cheerfully.

"I'm not here for 'hi's," she said. "Today is a pivotal moment in my life. You see, Jeremy's band is going to play at the festival. Jeremy is going to see me in the crowd. Not just because I have front-row seats, but because I'm going

to be cheering harder than anyone else. Like this."

Candace jumped around and waved her arms. "*Woo!* Yeah! *Woo,* baby! Oh, yeah! Sing it!"

She stopped cheering and turned to her brothers. "Then we're going to date through high school and college, marry, and have two kids, Xavier and Amanda," she said.

Candace daydreamed for a moment. Then she snapped back to reality.

"So don't you dare ruin it with one of your little project thingies!" she warned Phineas.

"No problem, Candace," Phineas said. "'Cause today we're doing nothing anyway."

"And don't try to give me—" Candace stopped. "Did you say 'nothing'?"

"Nothing," Phineas repeated, nodding.

"Nothing?" She gasped in disbelief.

"Nothing," Phineas said.

"Standing is something," Candace pointed out.

Just then, both Phineas and Ferb fell backward until they were lying on the grass, staring up at the sky.

"*Hmm.*" Candace had to admit that her brothers didn't seem to be doing anything. Of course, it wasn't even lunchtime yet.

"Well, you can't do nothing forever!" she snapped. "And when you stop doing nothing,

I'll start doing something—and that something will be busting you!"

Candace stomped into the house and watched Phineas and Ferb through a window. They weren't moving. But Candace wasn't going to be fooled by that!

"Look at them plotting my downfall," she muttered.

She pulled out her cell phone and dialed.

When Mrs. Flynn-Fletcher's phone rang, she was standing in her booth at the county fair. She was surrounded by stacks of handmade tea cozies. Each one was the perfect size to put over a teapot to keep the tea warm. Candace's mom had already sold a few, and she was hoping for a busy day. Then her cell phone rang.

"Hello?" she said.

"Mom!" Candace said. "Phineas and Ferb are doing nothing. Nothing! In a relentless effort to ruin my day!"

"Candace, honey," her mother said with a sigh, "why can't you just relax and let your brothers enjoy their do-nothing day?"

Candace hesitated. It would be nice to be able to kick back for once. Spying on her brothers in order to get them in trouble was hard work.

"Could it really be possible?" she said to herself. "Could Phineas and Ferb actually be doing nothing?"

She decided to take a chance. "You're right, Mom," she said. "I should just try and relax until Stacy picks me up for the concert."

"Exactly!" her mom said. "Love ya."

Candace hung up. "Well, if they really are doing nothing, I guess I've got some time to go about my own personal business," she said to herself. "Let's see, what do I usually do? I know!"

She flipped her cell phone open. "I'll call Stacy and tell her how I'm busting Phineas and Ferb for—"

She stopped talking and closed her cell phone.

"Oh, yeah," she said. "Can't do that, 'cause they're not doing anything." Then she had an idea. "Wait a minute! I know."

Candace set up the family's video camera in front of a window that looked into the backyard. "I'll put this camera in just the right spot so when Phineas and Ferb are—"

Then she remembered. Phineas and Ferb weren't doing anything. Which meant she couldn't catch them doing something!

Candace groaned with frustration and tried

again. "And then when Phineas and Ferb walk by," she said, "I'll—"

Her voice trailed off. She grunted, annoyed. Then Candace trudged to her bedroom to get ready for the concert.

A moment later, she stood in front of a mirror, carefully putting on lipstick.

"Well, if there's one thing I know," she said, "I'm going to look so good when I bust them for—"

Oh. Right. There was nothing to bust them for. She growled with irritation.

"Face it!" she said. "You can't do anything unless you're trying to bust them for doing

something! And if they're doing nothing, then . . ."

She wailed loudly. "Who is Candace?"

In the backyard, Phineas and Ferb hadn't moved. Lying in the grass, Phineas sighed as he looked up at the sunny sky, completely relaxed.

Then the sun was blocked out by a piece of paper. Phineas realized Candace was holding a building-plan diagram in front of his and Ferb's faces.

"Hey, Phineas," Candace said in an upbeat tone, "is it the perfect day to build one of these, or what?"

"Sorry, Candace," Phineas said. "It's like we said. We're pursuing the best do-nothing day ever. But if you put it in our inbox, we'll try to build it tomorrow."

Candace frowned and crumpled the paper. She pulled out another diagram and

79

waved that in
front of their
eyes.

"Huh? Huh?
Time-traveling
submarine?"
she said in a coaxing voice. "Come on!"

"Candace, now you're just taking pages from our project book," Phineas said.

His sister glanced down at the book she was holding. The words *Phineas and Ferb's Project Journal* were written on the front cover. She turned red and quickly hid the book behind her back.

Since Candace's attempts to get Phineas and Ferb back to their scheming ways had failed, she went back into the house. She sat down on the couch in the living room and picked up the TV remote.

"How can I inspire them to build something?" she wondered aloud as she turned on the TV.

Just then, a commercial appeared on-screen.

"Are you a boy?" a TV announcer asked. "Doing nothing with your stepbrother today? Do you like high adventure?"

"Yeah!" a crowd of kids on the TV yelled.

"Then we have the product for you!" the announcer went on. "It's the Amazing Man-Eating-Dinosaur–Themed Totally Sick Waterslide of Doom! That's right, kids. The Amazing Man-Eating-Dinosaur–Themed Totally Sick Waterslide of Doom can be delivered in just minutes!"

On-screen, a truck stopped in front of a house, and boxes were unloaded.

"And it's so easy to assemble, even a five-year-old can build it!" said the announcer.

"I did it!" said a cute kid on TV.

"Call now!" the announcer finished.

Candace didn't have to be told twice. She was already reaching for her phone.

Chapter 3

A short time later, a deliveryman unloaded a number of boxes into the Flynn-Fletchers' backyard. When he had finished, Candace signed for the shipment, smiling happily.

"Well, that's the last of it," the deliveryman said. "By the way, aren't you a little too old to be building one of these?" he asked, raising his eyebrows.

"Why, yes," Candace said. "Yes, I am."

Once the deliveryman had left, she started opening the boxes. "Okay, I'll get this thing started," she said. "And then, because they're men, they'll want to take over and show me how to do it. Then I'll call Mom and bust them!"

Happily, Candace unpacked the boxes.

Meanwhile, Perry was busy tracking down Dr. Doofenshmirtz. Perry knew he was up to something—but what? The scientist was a madman, but he was a brilliant madman. He had built his own evil empire, a company called Doofenshmirtz Evil, Inc. The offices were in a high-rise building topped with a company sign, so Perry knew exactly where to find Dr. Doofenshmirtz.

When Perry arrived, he kicked the door open and entered the building.

Dr. Doofenshmirtz looked up from his latest invention. He didn't seem upset to

see Perry. In fact, he seemed pleased.

"Oh, hello, Perry the Platypus," he said, smirking. "I'd like to introduce you to something."

He quickly turned around and pointed an unusual-looking machine at Perry. "My Slow-Motion-inator!" Dr. Doofenshmirtz cried as he pressed a button.

Zap! A ray from the machine hit Perry. He tried to run toward Dr. Doofenshmirtz, but he could only move in slow motion!

Dr. Doofenshmirtz watched Perry run at a snail's pace. He walked over and put one hand on Perry's head. Then Dr. Doofenshmirtz leaned on him, as if he were resting.

"This way you're too slow to foil my evil scheme, and I don't have to worry about capturing you," Dr. Doofenshmirtz explained. "Problem solved. Anyway, let's get down to business."

Perry may have been in slow-motion, but

he was determined to accomplish his mission. He kept running as Dr. Doofenshmirtz talked.

"I don't know if you've ever noticed, but I'm not exactly very . . . *hmm*, what do the kids call it these days?" Dr. Doofenshmirtz paused. "Ah, handsome. My doctor says it's genetic, but I don't blame my parents. I blame everyone else in the entire tri-state area for being better looking than me! So, I invented this: my Ugly-inator!"

He pulled out a machine that was bigger than the Slow-Motion-inator. This machine

was bright green with a plastic dome on the top. Inside the dome sat a frog, which gave a sad little croak.

"It harnesses the horned frog's unpleasant appearance to render its target ugly!" said Dr. Doofenshmirtz. The frog looked at him, annoyed, but the scientist didn't notice. "Let me give you a demonstration on handsome movie actor Vance Ward."

Dr. Doofenshmirtz pulled a rope, which lifted a sheet to reveal a man strapped to a board. He had thick, wavy blond hair, bright blue eyes, and perfect teeth. He was wearing an elegant suit.

Vance Ward smiled as if he were onstage and the curtain had just gone up.

"Hi! I'm Vance Ward," he said with a big smile.

"If it can turn him ugly, it can turn anything ugly," Dr. Doofenshmirtz said. "Are you ready, Vance?"

"I guess, but I didn't get a script," Vance said. "I mean, what's my motivation in this scene?"

"Motivation?" Dr. Doofenshmirtz said with a smirk. "Oh, I think it will be clear to you in a second."

He aimed the Ugly-inator at Vance and pulled the trigger. Immediately, the handsome actor turned into a misshapen, odd-looking man. He was wearing an undershirt and sagging pants.

Dr. Doofenshmirtz laughed. "Now, on to the rest of the tri-state area!" he cried. "Oh, and Perry the Platypus, you know what the best part of my plan is?"

* * *

A short while later, Dr. Doofenshmirtz had forced Perry and Vance onto a large platform that was attached to a huge balloon. When the top of the building opened, they floated up into the sky. On the platform was a reclining chair and a TV.

"I'm going to do it from the comfort of my own living room, with my favorite flat-screen TV and recliner," Dr. Doofenshmirtz said to Perry.

Perry tried to run toward Dr. Doofenshmirtz, but he was still in slow motion.

The evil scientist leaned back in the recliner

and put his hands behind his head. This was the life, he thought. Kicking back, relaxing, and doing nothing—except evil, of course!

In their yard, Phineas and Ferb were still lying on the grass. They were enjoying doing nothing. It was a refreshing change of pace.

Just then, Candace walked past them carrying an armful of boxes.

"Oh, hey, boys. I see you're still doing nothing," she said. "Oh, don't mind me. I'm just carrying a few construction supplies for a really huge, supercool contraption." She laughed. "You know, like the ones you used to build. Well, I figured I'd get in on the fun today."

She leaned over Phineas to pound a stake into the ground with a mallet.

"Oh, pardon my reach," she said. "Just trying to get into the most convenient position to drive this stake into the ground. Oh, yeah! I'm really having fun now!"

"Uh, Candace?" Phineas said.

"Oh, I know what you're going to say," she said, pleased. "Of course you can take over the whole operation."

"Uh, actually, I was going to ask if you could keep the noise down," Phineas said politely.

Candace frowned. She couldn't believe that Phineas wasn't taking the bait. No matter— she had a few more tricks up her sleeve!

"Uh, well, back to the important things in life, like having fun," she said.

She pulled out a jackhammer and started drilling into a beam. "Remember when you used to have this much fun?"

91

Phineas and Ferb ignored their sister.

A moment later, a mixing truck pulled up and started pouring cement in the backyard.

"All this fun could be yours, too," Candace said to her brothers.

Then a crane arrived. It began to move the dinosaur she'd ordered onto the yard.

"All you have to do is join me!" Candace said.

After a short time, Candace had nearly finished putting together the Amazing Man-Eating-Dinosaur–Themed Totally Sick

Waterslide of Doom. The slide came out of the dinosaur's mouth and twisted around before it reached the ground.

Sitting on the top of the waterslide, Candace was fastening a few last bolts to the dinosaur's head.

"I don't want to brag, but fun loves me more than it loves you right now!" Candace called to her brothers. She was annoyed that they hadn't tried to take over the project as she had planned.

Candace's cell phone was sitting next to her on the waterslide. But she didn't hear it ring over the noise of the machinery.

On Dr. Doofenschmirtz's floating platform, Perry felt as if he'd been running for hours in slow motion. Finally, he had almost reached his goal.

The Ugly-inator was on a table next to the recliner, where Dr. Doofenshmirtz was sitting. Perry stretched out his arm to grab the machine.

Just as Perry was about to pick up the Ugly-inator, Dr. Doofenshmirtz grabbed it.

"*Ooh!*" the scientist said with a laugh. He jumped up and began running around the platform, holding the machine. "Yoo-hoo, Perry the Platypus! Come and get it! Oh, I forgot. You're too slow to catch me now!"

What Dr. Doofenshmirtz didn't realize was that Perry had just laid a very clever trap—and the scientist had walked right into it!

As soon as Dr. Doofenshmirtz stepped away from the Slow-Motion-inator, Perry grabbed it. He grabbed it very slowly, but he still managed to get it before the scientist.

"Duh! Of course," Dr. Doofenshmirtz cried. "You were going for the Slow-Motion-inator."

Perry pointed the machine at himself.

"Wait! Wait, no!" yelled Dr. Doofenshmirtz. "Don't touch the reverse switch!"

At that moment, that's exactly what Perry did. The ray from the machine reversed the slow-motion effect.

Perry was back up to speed! He began

chasing Dr. Doofenshmirtz around the platform.

The scientist tried to aim the Ugly-inator at Perry as he ran. He missed several times. Finally, the Ugly-inator ray hit Perry in the head!

Suddenly, Perry no longer looked like his usual platypus self. His teeth were crooked, his eyes were different sizes, and his arms were weirdly shaped.

That's when Dr. Doofenshmirtz made a big mistake. He stopped to point and laugh.

"You should see yourself. You're so ugly!" he called.

Perry leaped into the air and kicked the Ugly-inator from the scientist's hand.

Then Perry picked up the machine and aimed it at the TV. It turned from a sleek flat panel to an old-fashioned TV with an antenna. Next, he aimed at the recliner. It turned into a plastic garden chair.

Shocked, Dr. Doofenshmirtz staggered back, accidentally hitting a switch with his elbow.

Instantly, an anchor dropped from the platform. It was headed right for the backyard where Phineas and Ferb were relaxing!

Chapter 4

In the Flynn-Fletchers' backyard, Candace continued to work, and her brothers continued to relax. Just then, Stacy walked into the yard.

"Candace, where are you?" Stacy yelled. "It's time to go!"

She looked up and saw Candace on top of the waterslide, still hammering. Stacy gasped. She had never seen her friend doing major construction work before.

"Candace?" Stacy said, shocked.

"Who's having fun now?!" Candace yelled at her brothers. She hadn't heard Stacy. "It's like boredom is a bad rash, and I'm a shot of cortisone."

Stacy climbed the slide's ladder, hoping to calm her friend down.

"Candace, what are you doing?" Stacy asked. "I've been trying to call you all afternoon!"

"What does it look like?" Candace snapped. "I'm busting my brothers!" She pointed to Phineas and Ferb, who were still lying peacefully on their backs.

"But the concert's starting right now!" Stacy pointed to the fairgrounds in the distance.

Candace's mouth dropped open. "Jeremy!" she said. "Oh, my gosh, I spent so much time busting my brothers, I forgot about the concert."

Just then, the anchor from the platform dropped into the backyard. It hooked onto the dinosaur's nostril. As the balloon carrying the platform drifted away, the Amazing Man-Eating-Dinosaur–Themed Totally Sick Waterslide of Doom was pulled off the ground.

Startled, the girls realized that the water-slide they were sitting on was floating in the air.

"Candace, what's happening?" Stacy asked.

"It didn't say anything in the instructions about being lifted up in the air!" Candace said, confused.

"*Aaahh!*" Both girls screamed.

At the summer festival, Jeremy and his band were onstage. They were performing one of their songs.

Jeremy sang lead vocals into a microphone as the audience watched.

Far above them, the balloon pulling the platform and the waterslide flew past. Perry and Dr. Doofenshmirtz were still fighting over the Ugly-inator. Then, they accidentally pressed its lever. An Ugly-inator ray hit the band onstage.

Suddenly, Jeremy had long, shaggy hair and was wearing a horned helmet on his head. His bandmates were wearing ripped clothes in dark colors, and their music was loud heavy metal.

The crowd cheered. Then an Ugly-inator

ray hit them, too. Instantly, they were transformed into people with spiky mohawks, multiple earrings, and black clothes.

A moment later, the anchor rope broke. The dinosaur waterslide plunged toward the stage!

"Aahhh!" Candace and Stacy screamed again.

Crash! The waterslide smashed onto the stage.

Jeremy and his band kept playing.

"Who are these guys?" Candace asked Stacy. She didn't recognize Jeremy or his bandmates.

Stacy shrugged. "They must be the opening act."

High above them, Perry finally wrestled the Ugly-inator from Dr. Doofenshmirtz. He took aim, and the ray hit the scientist in the face!

"Oh, no!" Dr. Doofenshmirtz cried. He grabbed his head with his hands. "Now *I'm* ugly!"

He lowered his hands and looked at them carefully. He realized that even after being shot with the Ugly-inator he still looked exactly the same.

"Oh. Oh, I get it," he said bitterly. *"Hardy-har-har."*

Perry opened the plastic dome on the top of the Ugly-inator and freed the frog. Then he put a photo inside the dome.

"My autographed picture of Vance Ward?" Dr. Doofenshmirtz cried. *"Ooh!* You've per-verted my ugly invention with something beautiful!"

Perry aimed the machine at Vance. *Zap!* The actor turned back into his former handsome self.

"Thanks!" Vance said. "Whoever you are . . ." Then he realized where he was. "Now get me out of here!" he shouted.

Instead, Perry pointed the machine at Jeremy and his heavy metal band. *Zap!* They

turned back into Jeremy and the Incidentals, crooning the sweet song they had started with.

Then Perry zapped the audience. Everyone in the crowd changed back into their regular selves.

Finally, Perry zapped himself. Once again, he was secret-agent Perry.

Dr. Doofenshmirtz scowled. "What about my TV and chair?" he demanded.

"Get me off this thing!" Vance suddenly yelled. He took a running leap off the edge of the platform and plummeted through the air.

Perry rolled his eyes. Some people don't understand the difference between real life and a movie, he thought. He jumped after the actor and managed to grab on to him. He shot them both with the Slow-Motion-inator. They fell slowly and gently to Earth.

As they fell, Perry pointed the machine that was previously the Ugly-inator at Dr. Doofenshmirtz's balloon. It turned into a huge, heart-shaped balloon that read: I LOVE GOODNESS.

"My balloon!" Dr. Doofenshmirtz cried in despair. How could he, an evil madman, be seen with a balloon that was so sweet? "Curse you, Perry the Platypus!" he shouted.

Perry had saved the world from the evil scientist once again, and made everything a little prettier, too.

At the end of the day, Mrs. Flynn-Fletcher closed up her tea-cozy booth and returned home. When she walked into the backyard, Phineas and Ferb were lying on the grass.

"Hey, boys, I'm home. Oh, I see you're still

enjoying your do-nothing day," said Mrs. Flynn-Fletcher.

"Yeah, Mom," Phineas said. "It was the best lazy day ever." He saw his pet platypus trot across the yard, followed by Vance. "Oh, there you are, Perry!" Phineas called.

Vance was still stuck in slow motion. "Where am I?" he asked. He was speaking very slowly, too.

"And with handsome movie actor Vance Ward," Ferb said, puzzled. "He seems much faster on TV."

Phineas and Ferb laid back down on the grass. It had been the best do-nothing day ever.

Back at the festival, Jeremy and the Incidentals were still performing onstage. The

crowd had applauded so much, Jeremy and his band were playing an encore.

Candace was still onstage, too. After the waterslide had crashed, she and Stacy had watched Jeremy and his band perform. Now Jeremy turned and smiled at Candace. She smiled back, then she joined in, singing along.

Candace and Jeremy sang the last few lines of the song together.

"This is the best day ever!" Candace cried happily. She and Jeremy were together at last—even if only for one song.

Don't miss the fun in the next
Phineas and Ferb book . . .

DAREDEVIL DAYS

Adapted by Molly McGuire
Based on the series created by Dan Povenmire & Jeff "Swampy" Marsh

Phineas and Ferb are building a skating rink
in their backyard for their grandma Betty Jo,
who used to be a roller-derby queen. Then
they find out that their friend Jeremy Johnson's
grandma used to be Grandma Betty Jo's
skating rival! Phineas and Ferb decide to hold
a contest to see which granny can roll to the
finish line the fastest! The thrills continue
when the boys help their grandpa Reg achieve
his lifelong dream of doing a stunt jump over
McGregor's Gorge!